# THE LEGEND OF
# SLEEPY HLLOW

## RiP VAN WiNKLE
## THE SPECTRE BRiDEGROOM

# WASHINGTON IRVING

Condensed and Adapted by

### W.T. ROBINSON
### KATHRYN R. KNIGHT

Illustrated by

### ALASTAIR GRAHAM

bendon

The Junior Classics have been
adapted and illustrated with care and thought
to introduce you to a world of famous authors, characters, ideas,
and great stories that have been loved for generations.

Editor — Kathryn Knight
Creative Director — Gina Rhodes Haynes
And the entire classics project team

THE LEGEND OF SLEEPY HOLLOW
RIP VAN WINKLE
THE SPECTRE BRIDEGROOM

Copyright © 2014 Bendon
Ashland, Ohio 44805 • 1-888-5-BENDON
bendonpub.com

Cover design by Mary Katherine Ethridge


Printed in the United States of America

# FOREWORD

*A note to the reader—*

Three classic stories rest in your hands. The characters are famous. The tales are timeless.

This Junior Classic edition of *The Legend of Sleepy Hollow*, *Rip Van Winkle*, and *The Spectre Bridegroom* has been carefully condensed and adapted from the original versions (which you really *must* read when you're ready for every detail). We kept the well-known phrases for you. We kept Washington Irving's style. And we kept the important imagery and heart of each tale.

Literature is terrific fun! It encourages you to think. It helps you dream. It is full of heroes and villains, suspense and humor, adventure and wonder, and new ideas. It introduces you to writers who reach out across time to say: "Do you want to hear a story I wrote?"

Curl up and enjoy.

# CONTENTS

# THE LEGEND OF
# SLEEPY HOLLOW

## RiP VAN WiNKLE
## THE SPECTRE BRiDEGROOM

# CONTENTS

# CHARACTERS

**ICHABOD CRANE** — the thin, odd-looking schoolteacher of Sleepy Hollow, who has his eye on Katrina Van Tassel—and her father's farm

**KATRINA VAN TASSEL** — the pretty, young flirt of Sleepy Hollow

**BALTUS VAN TASSEL** — Katrina's wealthy father, who gives a harvest feast

**BROM BONES** — the manly prankster of the area, who also has his eye on Katrina

**HANS VAN RIPPER** — a farmer who loans Ichabod his horse and his best saddle

**GUNPOWDER** — the horse Ichabod borrows to go to the Van Tassel feast

**DAREDEVIL** — Brom Bones' spirited black horse (his favorite)

**HEADLESS HORSEMAN** — the ghostly rider who is said to haunt Sleepy Hollow

# CHAPTER ONE

## A Sleepy Little Valley

In a large cove along the shore of the Hudson River there is a small market town called Tarry Town. The town looks out on a wide part of the river known as the Tappan Zee. Dutch sailors discovered this place many years ago, but they did not name it. The good housewives of the area named it. They called it Tarry Town because their husbands used to stop to talk and waste time, or "tarry," outside the village inn. I cannot say if this is the real truth, but it *is* what I was told.

Not far from this village there is a little valley among high hills. It is one of the quietest and most peaceful places in the whole world.

# THE LEGEND OF
# SLEEPY HOLLOW

# THE LEGEND OF SLEEPY HOLLOW

A burbling brook runs through it with a soft, sleepy sound. All you hear in this valley are the whistles of quails and the tapping woodpeckers. When I was a young boy, I used to hunt squirrels in the tall walnut trees that shade one side of the valley. The sound of my gun rang through the woods and echoed through the still valley. I know of no better place to get away from the rest of the world and dream.

Because of the lazy quiet of this valley, it has long been known as Sleepy Hollow. A dreamy feeling hangs over the land and drifts through the air. Some say that a German doctor put a curse on the place. Others say that an old Indian chief— the wizard of his tribe—held his pow-wows there. (That would have been *long* before Henry Hudson explored this part of New York State.) But one thing *is* for sure. The place still seems to hold the people under a spell. They believe in all sorts of superstitions. They often see strange sights or hear music and voices in the air. Stars and comets blaze across the valley. And night-mares play their tricks on the people's minds. The whole neighborhood is rich with ghost stories and haunted spots.

# THE LEGEND OF
# SLEEPY HOLLOW

The thing that most often haunts this valley is a phantom on horseback—*without a head*. Some people say it is the ghost of a soldier whose head had been shot away during the Revolutionary War. They see him hurrying along in the gloom of night, as if on the wings of the wind. He haunts the valley, and also the roads, especially the area around a nearby church.

The story goes that the body of this phantom had been buried in the churchyard. Its ghost rides out at night in search of his head. They say that he rushes through Sleepy Hollow like a midnight tornado, in a hurry to get back to the churchyard before sunrise. The people of the little village gather around their fireplaces and tell wild tales about this ghostly thing. It is known as the *Headless Horseman of Sleepy Hollow*.

I should tell you one more thing. The people who live in Sleepy Hollow see and hear these mysterious things—yes. But everyone who comes to *stay* in that sleepy area begins to dream dreams and see ghosts, too. It is almost as if there is something bewitching in the air they breathe.

# CHAPTER TWO

# Ichabod Crane

Long ago in this valley there lived a man by the name of Ichabod Crane. He came from Connecticut and stayed for a time in Sleepy Hollow as its schoolmaster.

Ichabod looked a lot like a crane bird. He was tall and very thin with narrow shoulders and long arms and legs. His hands dangled a mile out of his sleeves. His feet were the size of shovels. His head was small and flat on top. He had huge ears, large green glassy eyes, and a long pointed nose. If you saw his loose, floppy body on a windy day, with his baggy clothes fluttering about, you'd think it was a scarecrow from a cornfield.

# THE LEGEND OF
# SLEEPY HOLLOW

He taught in a squat, one-room schoolhouse built of rough logs. Many of the windows were broken and stuffed with pages of old books to keep the weather out. It was in a lonely but pleasant place, at the foot of a wooded hill with a brook running close by.

On sleepy summer days, the low hum of his students' voices sounded like bees in a hive. Now and then this buzz was broken by the firm voice of the schoolmaster. Sometimes there came the awful sound of the birch rod on the backside of some lazy student who needed to be "helped along" with his lessons. Ichabod always kept in mind the saying: *Spare the rod and spoil the child*. Ichabod Crane certainly did *not* spoil his children!

Yet he was not one of those *mean* teachers who *enjoyed* punishing. He was choosy about whom to spank. The boys who ran in fear from him usually got away without a smack. But the tough little rascals who talked back to him were sure to feel the stinging birch rod. He called this: "doing their parents a favor." Whenever he gave a spanking, he promised the child: "You'll remember this and thank me for it as long as you live." (For some reason, the rascals never thanked him.)

When school hours were over, however, Ichabod Crane was the friend and playmate of the students. On holiday afternoons, he walked some of the smaller children home—especially if they had pretty older sisters, or mothers who were good cooks.

Ichabod had a reason for being friendly with his students and their parents. His pay as a teacher was very low. It was not enough to feed *him*. For, even though he was thin, he was *always* hungry. To make up for his low pay, parents let him live with them on their farm for a week at a time. (He could put everything he owned in a little cloth bundle.) And so, at least he had food and a place to sleep as he moved from place to place around the neighborhood.

Most of the people he stayed with still thought he was paid too much. They thought school-masters were just lazy loafers. To keep them happy, Ichabod helped with the work around the homes. He cut and raked hay, mended the fences, took the horses to water, drove the cows from pasture, and cut wood for the winter fire. The children thought he was much nicer around the farms than he was at the schoolhouse.

He made the mothers happy by cuddling the younger children. He would sit with a child on one knee, and rock a cradle with his foot hour after hour.

Ichabod also earned a little extra money as the singing teacher of the neighborhood. On Sundays, he was very proud to stand at the front of the church with his group of singers. He was quite sure *he* was more important than even the preacher. One thing *was* sure—his voice was the loudest in the whole church. (In fact, to this day, on quiet Sunday mornings there are still strange, warbling sounds that come from that church. The people say they are echoes of sounds that had once passed through the long nose of Ichabod Crane.)

The schoolmaster is an important man among the ladies of a country village. They see him as a gentleman. They think the schoolmaster is more polite and smarter than the rough farm boys, and almost as smart as the preacher. Oh, how they would fuss when Ichabod Crane came to eat at their farmhouse! Most of the time, the ladies put out an extra dish of cakes or candy, or their best silver teapot.

# THE LEGEND OF
# SLEEPY HOLLOW

# THE LEGEND OF
# SLEEPY HOLLOW

Ichabod liked the smiles of all the young ladies and tried his best to please them. How happy he made them in the churchyard on Sundays. He gathered grapes for them from the wild vines that grew in the trees. He entertained them by reading all the messages on the tombstones. He took them for walks along the banks of the nearby pond. The shy country boys just stood back and watched, wishing *they* were half as clever.

# THE LEGEND OF SLEEPY HOLLOW

Ichabod moved around so much that he became a kind of traveling newspaper. The people were always glad to see him and hear all the stories and gossip he carried from house to house. The women thought he was well educated, for he had read several books all the way through. He told them about one book called *History of New England Witchcraft*, written by Cotton Mather. And he himself believed its scary tales of witches and their spells.

He became more interested in mysterious things the longer he lived in Sleepy Hollow. No tale was too wild or strange for him to believe. After school, he loved to lie on the grass next to the little brook that ran by his schoolhouse and study all the frightful tales of witchcraft in Cotton Mather's book. When night came and he could no longer see to read, he headed off through dark swamps and lonely forests to the farmhouse where he was living. Every sound of nature, at that witching hour, played tricks on his mind:

The moan of the whippoorwill from the hillside!

The cry of the tree toad!

The hooting of the screech owl!

The sudden flapping wings of birds frightened from the bushes!

Everything startled him—even the fireflies, which sparkled so brightly in the darkest places, and flew in front of his face. And if a huge beetle came flying into him, poor Ichabod was scared out of his wits! Was it a witch's sign? The only way he knew to calm his fears or drive away evil spirits was to sing church songs. The people of Sleepy Hollow often listened in wonder to tunes floating from a distant hill, or along a dark road.

# THE LEGEND OF
# SLEEPY HOLLOW

Ichabod also liked to spend long winter evenings with the old Dutch wives, listening to their tales of ghosts and goblins. They told of haunted fields, and haunted brooks, and haunted bridges, and haunted houses, and always of the Headless Horseman. He would share what he had read of witchcraft, and tell about the scary sights and sounds that had gone on long ago in Connecticut. Sometimes he frightened them with his ideas about comets and shooting stars. He even got them to believe that the world did not turn all the way around, and that, half the time, they were upside down!

But all good things must end. Before long, the evening in the cozy room by the crackling wood fire was over. Then he had to face the terrors of his lonely walk home. What awful shapes and scary shadows crossed his path on a dark, snowy night! How he wished he were back in that warm room. Snow-covered bushes, like ghosts dressed in white sheets, seemed to jump in front of him! He would shrink with terror at the sound of his own steps on the frosty crust under his feet. He was afraid to look over his shoulder, thinking he might see some beast sneaking up behind him!

# THE LEGEND OF
# SLEEPY HOLLOW

# THE LEGEND OF
# SLEEPY HOLLOW

And when a rushing blast of wind howled through the trees, he thought it was the Headless Horseman on one of his night rides!

But these were only the terrors of the night. During the day things were just fine. And he would have had a pleasant life if his path had not been crossed by something that causes more mystery to man than all the ghosts, goblins, and witches put together. And that was—a woman.

# CHAPTER THREE

# Katrina Van Tassel

One of Ichabod Crane's music students was Katrina Van Tassel. She was the daughter and only child of a rich Dutch farmer. Katrina was just eighteen and pretty as a picture. You might say she was as ripe and rosy-cheeked as one of her father's peaches. She was also a flirt! She wore the type of fancy clothing that would best show off her beauty. Her petticoats were always *just* short enough to show the prettiest foot and ankle Ichabod had ever seen.

Ichabod Crane had a soft heart toward the ladies, so it is not surprising that he liked such a beautiful girl as Katrina. He liked her even more

# THE LEGEND OF
# SLEEPY HOLLOW

when he saw her father's huge mansion. Katrina's father, Baltus Van Tassel, was one of the richest farmers in the whole area. His expensive home was located on the banks of the Hudson. A great elm tree spread its broad branches over it. At the foot of the tree, a spring of the softest and sweetest water bubbled up in a little well and then sparkled away through the grass to a nearby brook. Next to the farmhouse was a wonderful, large barn.

The rich treasures of the farm were everywhere. Swallows swooped and twittered around in the air. Rows of cooing pigeons were enjoying the sunshine on the roof. Fat pigs were grunting in the peace of their large pens, while their babies followed them around, snuffing at the air. Geese and ducks were floating on a nearby pond. Turkeys were gobbling through the farmyard. A proud rooster marched around in front of the barn door, like a fine gentleman. He clapped his wings and crowed with pride. He scratched and tore up the earth with his feet, and then called his hungry family of hen-wives and chick-children to enjoy the treat he had found for them.

The schoolmaster's mouth watered as he looked at all these wonderful things to eat. He could imagine them all cooked up for a fine feast. A young pig, tender and juicy, with an apple in its mouth. Sides of bacon and ham. Pigeons put to bed in a tasty potpie. Geese and ducks swimming in gravy. He imagined every turkey sewn up and stuffed with spicy dressing. And the rooster lay flat on his back on a platter—his drumsticks sticking straight up.

Still dreaming of food, Ichabod's great green eyes rolled over the beautiful Van Tassel estate. All around him were rich fields of wheat, rye, buckwheat, and Indian corn, and orchards heavy with ripe fruit. His heart longed for the young Katrina. For, someday, when her parents died, all of this would belong to her. And if he could make her his wife, it would also belong to *him*.

Ichabod saw how he could turn everything into cash. The money could be used to buy land and build palaces in the wilderness. He could see Katrina with a whole family of children, sitting on top of a wagon loaded with their household goods. And he saw himself riding a mare, with a colt at her heels, setting out to seek his fortune.

# THE LEGEND OF
# SLEEPY HOLLOW

When he walked up to the house, his desire for Katrina grew even stronger. It was one of those large farmhouses built in the style of the first Dutch settlers. There was a porch along the front, which could be closed up in bad weather. All around the porch hung farm tools, harnesses, bridles, and nets for fishing. Benches were built along the sides for summer use. There was a great spinning wheel at one end, and a butter churn at the other.

Ichabod left the porch and went into the pantry off the living room. Shelves full of expensive pewter shone before his eyes. In one corner stood a huge bag of wool, ready to be spun. In another corner he saw a pile of fine woven cloth, just taken from the loom. Ears of Indian corn and strings of dried apples, peaches, and bright red peppers decorated the walls.

He peeped into the parlor through a partly-open door. It was full of fancy chairs and dark mahogany tables that shone like mirrors. Dried fruit, shells, and colored birds' eggs hung above the fireplace. A great ostrich egg was hung from the center of the room. And a cupboard held rich treasures of old silver and fine china.

Ichabod's only thought now was how to win the heart of the Van Tassel daughter. This would be a hard task! This would be harder, even, than the most heroic tasks of the knights of old. The only things *they* had to face were giants and fiery dragons. All a *knight* had to do was get through gates of iron and brass and walls of stone to the castle room where the lady of his heart was held. Then the lady would agree to marry him, and they'd live happily ever after.

Ichabod, however, had a harder job. He had to win his way to the heart of a teasing country girl. And, oh, how she could change her mind from one day to the next! Not only that, he had to deal with all the other young men who were just as interested in Katrina as he was. They kept a watchful and angry eye on one another, but were ready to join together against someone new— like Ichabod.

# CHAPTER FOUR

# Brom Bones

Among these young men, the most difficult was a husky, reckless man by the name of Brom Van Brunt. He was the hero of the local countryside, known for his strength and daring. He was broad-shouldered and had short, curly black hair. He was rough—but not unpleasant. Because of his strength and the power of his arms and legs, he had the nickname of Brom Bones.

Brom Bones was famous for his great skill in riding horses, and in every other sport he tried. He was always ready for either a fight or a game, but he had more mischief than meanness in him.

# THE LEGEND OF
# SLEEPY HOLLOW

Under all his roughness, there was some playful good humor. He had three or four close friends who followed him around the country. They would show up at every fight or fun they could find.

In cold weather, Brom wore a fur cap with a flashy fox's tail on top. Whenever the folks at a country gathering spied this hat at a distance, they expected mischief of some kind. At times, his gang dashed along past the farmhouses at midnight, whooping and hollering. The old women, startled out of their sleep, would listen for a moment until the hurry-scurry had clattered by. Then they would say, "Aye, there goes Brom Bones and his gang!" And, whenever there was a silly prank or fight in the neighborhood, they shook their heads. They knew Brom Bones had something to do with it.

Brom Bones liked Katrina, too. Although he was about as tender and gentle as a bear, folks said she also liked *him*. Brom Bones' rivals had no desire to upset a lion (or a bear) in love. Whenever his horse was tied to Van Tassel's fence on a Sunday night, all the other young men passed by and went to visit other young ladies.

But Ichabod did not give in to Brom. Even a big, strong man like Brom Bones could not shake Ichabod's confidence. The tall, thin schoolmaster was like a steel spring. Though he bent under pressure, he never broke. He always popped back up with his head held high.

It would have been crazy to go up against Brom Bones face to face. Ichabod made his moves in a quiet, sly way.

His job as singing teacher gave him a chance to visit the farmhouse often. Katrina's parents didn't seem to mind. Balt Van Tassel loved his daughter better even than his pipe. He let her have her way in everything. His little wife, too, had enough to do taking care of her house and the poultry. As she wisely said: "Ducks and geese are foolish things and must be looked after. But girls can take care of themselves."

So, while Mrs. Van Tassel bustled around the house, or worked at her spinning wheel at one end of the porch, old Balt sat smoking his evening pipe at the other. In the meantime, Ichabod would sit with their daughter by the side of the spring under the big elm tree, or take walks with her in the twilight.

# THE LEGEND OF
# SLEEPY HOLLOW

As soon as Ichabod Crane began visiting Katrina, a bitter feud started between him and Brom Bones. Brom had a sense of honor. He wanted to settle things like the knights of old—in man-to-man combat. But Ichabod would not enter the field of battle against Brom. He had heard Bones brag, "I'll double the schoolmaster up, and lay him on a shelf of his own schoolhouse!" The schoolmaster was not going to give him a chance to do that.

When Ichabod would not meet him for a fight, Brom became upset. He and his gang began playing practical jokes on Ichabod. They smoked out his singing school by stopping up the chimney. Then they broke into the schoolhouse at night and turned everything upside down. The poor schoolmaster began to think all the witches in the country held their meetings there.

But what was still worse, Brom began making
a fool of Ichabod in front of Katrina. After
teaching his dog to whine with a most horrible
sound, Brom told Katrina that the animal would
be a better singing teacher than Ichabod.

Things went on this way for some time, with
no real changes between the two young men.
Then, one day, Ichabod Crane got a little bit of
good luck.

# The Life of Rip Van Winkle

Anyone who has traveled up the Hudson River north of New York City will remember the Catskill Mountains. They can be seen standing to the west of the river like proud kings looking over their land. In some ways the mountains are magic. They seem to change color and shape right before your eyes. Mostly, they change with the weather. When the weather is nice and clear, the mountains are dressed in blues and purples. At other times, clouds make circles of gray mist around their peaks. When the sun is going down and shines its rays on these misty circles, they look like golden halos on angel heads.

At the foot of these fairyland mountains, if you look closely, you might see smoke curling up from the houses of a small village. The roofs of the houses shine and sparkle among the trees just at the place where the blue hills meet the fresh greens of the fields and valleys. It is a little village of long ago. Dutch people came here from their homes in Holland, before the Revolutionary War against England. With the help of their good governor, Peter Stuyvesant, they formed a colony. They built their homes out of small yellow bricks brought from Holland, and it looked like a village of gingerbread houses.

In that same village, in one of these little houses, there lived many years ago (while the country was still ruled by England) a simple, happy fellow by the name of Rip Van Winkle. He was a part of the same Van Winkle family who, so many years before him, had fought brave and bloody battles in the army of Peter Stuyvesant. But Rip did not have the fighting character of his ancestors. I have already said that he was a simple, happy man. He was also a kind neighbor, and a man who obeyed his wife.

Rip Van Winkle's wife scolded and nagged at him day and night. Pick, pick, cluck, cluck, peck, peck, peck! Like an old mother hen, Mrs. Van Winkle never stopped. It was easy to see why he was known around the village as a hen-pecked husband. Maybe his troubles with his wife were what made him so gentle and well liked. Sometimes, men who are ruled by nagging wives at home are easy to get along with outside the walls of their houses. They seem to know how to be patient. A scolding wife may, therefore, be a blessing. If that is true, Rip Van Winkle was truly well blessed!

Rip was so well liked, that even the other wives of the village would stick up for him when he was scolded by his wife. And the children of the village would shout with joy whenever they saw him. He coached them in their sports, made their toys, taught them to fly kites and shoot marbles, and told them long stories about ghosts, witches, and Indians. When he walked through the village, they would hang on his clothing, climb on his back, and play a thousand tricks on him. And not a dog would bark at him when he passed by.

Rip did have one weakness. He didn't like to work at the things he was *supposed* to do. But he didn't mind staying busy doing other things. For instance, he would sit on a wet rock with a long heavy pole and fish all day, even when he got not one single bite. He would carry a gun on his shoulder for hours and tramp through woods and swamps to shoot a few squirrels or wild pigeons. He would help his neighbors with their work and run errands for the women of the village. In other words, he was ready to take care of anybody's work except his own. When it came to his own family matters and keeping his farm in good shape, he just could not do it.

In fact, he said it was of no use to work on his farm. It was the worst little piece of ground in the whole country. Everything about it went wrong. His fences were always falling to pieces. His cow would either get into cabbages or wander off. Weeds were sure to grow quicker in *his* fields than anywhere else. And the rain *always* began just as he had some outdoor work to do. He had not taken care of the farm his father had passed on to him. There was only a small patch of corn and potatoes left, and even that was in bad shape.

Rip Van Winkle's children were ragged and wild, too. They ran around the village as if they didn't even belong to anybody. His son, who was named after him, was also a lot like him. He followed like a puppy at his mother's heels, dressed in baggy old pants handed down from his father. He was always trying to hold them up with one hand, like a lady lifting her long dress to keep it out of mud puddles.

Rip Van Winkle was one of those people who looked for the easy way out of everything. He would rather starve with a penny in his pocket than work for a dollar. If it had been left up to him, he would have whistled life away in perfect peace. But it wasn't left up to him. His wife kept nagging at him about his laziness and the mess he was making of his family's life. Morning, noon, and night, her tongue went without stopping. Anything he said or did only made things worse. So he had gotten in the habit of just shrugging his shoulders, shaking his head, and saying nothing. But this would often make his wife angrier—and then Rip would give up and get out of the house.

Rip's only friend at home was his dog, Wolf. Wolf was as hen-pecked as Rip because Mrs. Van Winkle thought he was just as lazy as his master. She even looked at Wolf (with an evil eye) as the cause of Rip's bad habits. But, really, Wolf was a good dog, as brave an animal as ever hunted the woods—but not brave enough to face the anger of Mrs. Van Winkle. As soon as Wolf entered the house, his look became sad, his tail dropped to the ground or curled between his legs, and he sneaked about, trying to stay away from Mrs. Van Winkle. And just as soon—she would spot him! She would then wave a broom or even just a large spoon, and Wolf would run yelping to the door.

Times grew worse and worse for Rip Van Winkle as the years went on. When he could not stand to be scolded at home another minute, Rip tried to cheer himself up by finding some of his friends in the village. The men would meet on a bench in front of the inn. Above them hung the inn's sign, and on that sign was a painting of His Majesty King George of England. Here they sat in the shade through long, lazy summer days, talking over village gossip, or telling long, sleepy stories about nothing. Sometimes they would listen as Derrick Van Bummel, the schoolmaster, read to them from a newspaper that was a month old. Oh, how wise they thought they were as they argued about matters that had already been solved!

The group leader was an older man named Nicholas Vedder, who was also the owner of the inn. He sat at the inn door from morning to night, just moving every so often to stay in the shade of a large tree. He spoke little, but he smoked his pipe the whole time. The men could always tell what he was thinking by the way he smoked his pipe. When something upset him, he sent out short, angry puffs. When he was happy, he breathed in the smoke slowly, and let it out in light and peaceful clouds. And sometimes, taking the pipe from his mouth and letting the sweet smoke curl around his nose, he quietly nodded his head if he heard something he agreed with.

But Rip could not hide forever. Sooner or later, his scolding wife found him. She would rush into the meeting, shout at the men, and preach to them about their laziness.

There was only one way Rip knew of to get away from the work of the farm and screeching of his wife. If things got too bad, he would pick up his gun and walk away into the woods. Here he would sometimes sit down at the foot of a tree to share some food from his knapsack with Wolf.

"Poor Wolf," he would say, "your mistress treats you badly. But never mind, my lad. As long as I live, you shall always have a friend to stand by you!" Wolf would wag his tail and look sadly at his master's face. If a dog can feel sorry for someone, Wolf surely must have felt sorry for Rip.

# A Strange Game of Ninepins

During one of these walks in the woods, on a pretty fall day, Rip had climbed to one of the highest parts of the Catskill Mountains. He was enjoying his favorite sport of squirrel hunting. The quiet mountains had echoed and re-echoed with the explosions of his gun. By late in the afternoon he had become tired. When he came to a green, grassy hill at the top of a cliff, he sat down to rest.

Through an opening in the trees he could look across the countryside for many miles. He saw the mighty Hudson River far, far below him, moving on its silent, powerful way. The water was smooth as a mirror. Now and then he saw the reflection of a purple cloud or the sail of a boat sleeping on its glassy surface.

On the other side of the mountain he looked down into a deep mountain valley—wild, lonely, and tangled. Way down in the floor of the valley, lit by the faint rays of the setting sun, were tons of huge rocks that had tumbled down from the high cliffs. Evening was creeping in, and the mountains began to throw their long blue shadows over the valleys. Rip knew it would be dark long before he could reach the village. He shivered at the thought of having to face the anger of Mrs. Van Winkle.

As he was about to return down the mountain, he heard a voice from a distance, calling out, "Rip Van Winkle! Rip Van Winkle!" He looked around, but saw only one lone crow flying away across the mountain. He thought he was hearing things and turned again toward home. Then he heard the same cry ring through the quiet evening air: "Rip Van Winkle! Rip Van Winkle!" Wolf heard it, too. The hair on his back bristled up. He gave a low growl and slunk to his master's side. Rip felt a fear creeping over him.

Rip stared hard at the valley below. There he saw a strange figure slowly struggling up the rocks and bending under the heavy load of something he carried on his back. Rip was surprised to see anyone else in this lonely, distant place. But perhaps it was someone in trouble—so he hurried down to see if he could help.

As he came closer, he thought his eyes were playing tricks on him. What a strange-looking man! He was a short, square-built old fellow, with thick bushy hair and a straggly gray beard. His clothes looked like the ones the Dutch people wore a long time ago: a cloth vest strapped around the waist and baggy, knee-length trousers with rows of buttons down the sides and bunches at the knees. On his shoulder was a big barrel. He made signs for Rip to help him with the heavy load. Rip was afraid of the strange man at first and wasn't sure what to do. But, as I've told you, Rip was good about doing things for others. He agreed to help.

Taking turns with the barrel, the two men scrambled up a narrow, deep ditch, or gully, that had been dug out by a mountain stream. It was dry now—and full of rocks.

As they went on climbing, Rip heard long, rolling booms like distant thunder. The sounds were coming from a deep rock canyon—*and they were headed right toward it!* He stopped for a few seconds. He thought perhaps it was the rumbling of one of those passing thundershowers that often rattle around in mountains—so he went on.

They made it through the canyon and came to an open hollow with steep cliffs on every side. It looked like a giant outdoor theater carved right out of the mountain. Branches of trees hung over from the top edges of the cliffs, like a roof hiding the evening skies.

Rip and the stranger had not yet spoken one word. Rip wondered what the purpose could be of carrying a barrel up this wild mountain. But the mystery of it kept him from asking any questions.

As Rip entered the open hollow, he saw a more mysterious sight. On a level spot in the center of the hollow was a crazy-looking group of men playing the game of ninepins. They were dressed in an odd, old-fashioned style. Some wore short jackets, others vests. All had long knives in their belts. Most of them had huge, baggy trousers, just like the man who had led Rip up the mountain.

Their faces were unusual, too. One had a large beard, broad face, and small pig-like eyes. Another had a huge nose and wore a white, cone-shaped hat with a red feather sticking from its top. They all had beards of different shapes and colors.

There was one who seemed to be the leader— a large, powerful, old gentleman with a wrinkled face. He wore a laced-up leather jacket, broad belt, high-peaked hat with a feather, red stockings, and high-heeled shoes with roses in them. The whole group reminded Rip of the figures he had seen in an old painting of the earliest Dutch people of the village. How could that be?

Something else puzzled Rip. These folks, who should have been enjoying their party, were oddly silent and had the most serious faces. Rip thought they were the most unhappy-looking group of bowlers he had ever seen. The only sounds came from the noise of the balls. Whenever they were rolled, they echoed along the mountains like rumbling claps of thunder.

As Rip got nearer to the bowlers, they suddenly stopped their game and stared at him. They looked so unfriendly that his heart pounded in his chest and his knees knocked together.

Rip looked around for his companion. There he was—filling flagons from the barrel. He made signs to Rip to deliver the large glasses to the others, which Rip did with fear and trembling. The strange men drank with large gulps in complete silence, and then returned to their game of ninepins.

Little by little, Rip became less afraid. He even took a chance, when no one was watching, at filling a flagon and tasting the brew. He was naturally a thirsty person, and decided to try another—and another—and another. After many visits to the barrel he felt himself getting dizzy. Everything got fuzzy, his chin dropped down on his chest, and he fell into a deep sleep.

# Waking Up... to a Dream?

When Rip Van Winkle woke up, he found himself on the green, grassy hill where he had first seen the old man of the valley. He rubbed his eyes. It was a bright, sunny morning. The birds were chirping and hopping among the bushes. An eagle circled high above, gliding on the currents of the pure mountain breeze.

"Surely," thought Rip, "I have not slept here all night."

He tried to remember what happened before he fell asleep. The strange man with the barrel— the mountain canyon—the wild place among the rocks—the odd, unhappy bowlers—the drinks...

"Oh! Those drinks! That wicked barrel!" thought Rip. "What am I going to tell Mrs. Van Winkle?"

He looked around for his gun. It was nowhere in sight. Instead, he found an old, antique weapon lying by him. It was covered with rust, pieces were falling off, and the wooden parts were rotten and worm-eaten.

He now thought that the weird men of the mountain had played a trick on him with their strong drink. They had stolen his gun while he was asleep. Wolf was gone, too—he had probably wandered off to chase a squirrel or bird. Rip whistled to him and shouted his name. The echoes repeated his whistle and shout, but there was no sign of his old friend.

He decided to hunt the men down and get his dog and gun back. As he stood up to walk, he found himself stiff and sore.

"These mountain beds do not agree with me," thought Rip, "and if I get lame from this foolishness and can't work, I shall be in awful trouble with my wife."

He limped down into the valley and found the deep ditch that he had crossed the day before. But it wasn't dry anymore! A mountain stream was now rushing down it, leaping from rock to rock, filling the valley with babbling sounds.

He scrambled across the ditch and began crawling through a thick tangle of birch trees and twisted grapevines.

Finally he reached the place where the deep canyon had opened through the cliffs into the level "bowling alley." But now the opening was gone. Rip saw nothing but a huge, high wall of rocks. A rushing, foaming flood of water was crashing down the rocky sides into a deep, black pool. Rip stopped and again called and whistled for his dog. The only answer came from a cawing flock of crows, playing high in the air above his head. It seemed to Rip that they were making fun of him and his problems.

What was he going to do? It was now late in the morning, and he was hungry and in need of his breakfast. He felt terrible about the loss of his dog and gun. He was afraid to face his wife, but he couldn't just stay in the mountains and starve.

He shook his head and picked up the rusty gun. Full of sadness and worry, he turned toward home.

As he came near the village, he met a number of people, but he didn't know any of them. This surprised him, for he thought he had met everyone around there. Their clothing, too, was different from any he had seen. Everyone stared back at him. They seemed as surprised as he was. Whenever they looked at him, they pulled at their chins. Rip became curious and touched his own chin. When he did, he could not believe what he felt. His beard was a *foot long!*

When he got to the town center, a crowd of children he had never seen before began running at his heels. They teased him and pointed at his long, gray beard. Even the dogs were strangers to him and barked at him as he passed. The village was changed, too. It was much larger, with many more people. There were rows of houses that he had never seen before. The homes that he used to visit were gone. Strange names were over the doors—strange faces were at the windows—everything was strange.

His mind filled with questions. Were he and the village under some kind of witch's spell? Was this his same village, which he had left just the day before?

Off in the distance, Rip could see the Catskill Mountains and the silver Hudson River. Every hill and valley was in the right place. This had to be his own village! Rip's mind was spinning.

"That strong drink last night," he thought, "has befuddled and mixed up my poor head!"

After getting lost a few times, he finally found his way to his own house. He walked toward the porch with silent fear, waiting to hear his wife's scolding voice. Then he stopped.

He found the house in ruins. The roof had fallen in. The windows were broken out, and the doors were off the hinges. A half-starved dog that looked like Wolf was sneaking around. Rip called him by name, but the animal snarled, showed his teeth, and turned away. This hurt poor Rip.

"My own dog," he sighed "has forgotten me!"

Slowly, Rip entered the broken-down house, which Mrs. Van Winkle had always kept neat and clean. It was messy, lonely, and empty. He forgot his fears of punishment and called loudly for his wife and children. The lonely rooms rang for a moment with his voice, and then everything was silent again.

He rushed out and hurried to his old safe place, the village inn—but it was gone, too. In its place stood a large, broken-down, wooden building. Some of the broken windows were stuffed with old clothes to keep the weather out. Over the door was written: *The Union Hotel by Jonathan Doolittle.*

Instead of the big tree that used to shade the quiet little Dutch inn, there was now a tall flagpole. On the flag was a design of stars and stripes, which Rip had never before seen.

Rip did see the old inn sign, however, and the face of King George. But even this was different. The red coat was now blue with gold trim. A sword was held in the hand instead of a king's staff. The head wore a three-cornered hat, and underneath was painted in large letters:

## GENERAL
## GEORGE WASHINGTON

There was, as usual, a crowd of people around the door, but nobody that Rip knew. The people were busy talking and arguing. The sleepy talk that he remembered was gone.

Rip looked for the wise Nicholas Vedder, with his broad face, double chin, and long pipe, pumping out clouds of smoke. He looked for Van Bummel, the schoolmaster, reading from an old newspaper. In place of these, a restless-looking fellow was delivering angry speeches and passing out notices about *Rights of Citizens—Elections—Members of Congress—Liberty—Bunker's Hill—Heroes of the Year 1776*—none of which made any sense to Rip.

Rip, with his long, gray beard, his rusty gun, his style of clothes, and an army of women and children at his heels, soon got the attention of the people. They crowded around, looking him over from head to foot. The man who had been speaking rushed up to him and asked, "On which side did *you* vote?" and, "Are you a Federal or Democrat?"

Rip was still trying to figure out what all this could mean, when a proud old gentleman in a three-cornered hat made his way through the crowd, pushing folks to the right and left with his elbows. He stopped right in front of Rip, one hand on his hip, the other resting on his cane. He asked Rip what brought him to the election with a gun on his shoulder, and a mob at his heels, and whether he was going to start a riot in the village.

"Gentlemen," cried Rip, quite upset, "I am a poor, quiet man. I live here, and I am loyal to the King of England, God bless him!"

This brought loud, angry shouts from the crowd. "A friend of England! A spy! Put him in jail!" When the crowd quieted down, the man in the three-cornered hat asked again why he was there and whom he was looking for. Poor Rip told him that he meant no harm, but only came there looking for some of his friends who used to meet in front of the inn.

"Well—who are they? Name them."

Rip thought for a moment, and asked, "Where's Nicholas Vedder?"

There was silence for a little while. Then an old man answered in a thin, high voice, "Nicholas Vedder! Why, he's been dead these past eighteen years! There was a wooden tombstone in the cemetery that used to tell about him, but that's rotten and gone."

"Where's Brom Dutcher?" asked Rip.

"Oh, he went off to the army in the beginning of the war. Some say he was killed at the battle of Stony Point—others say he was drowned at sea. I don't know—he never came back again."

"Where's Van Bummel, the schoolmaster?"

"He went off to the wars, too. He was a great general, and is now a congressman."

Rip's heart was sad to hear about these changes in his home and friends. He felt alone in some new world. Every answer puzzled him. He knew nothing about any war, or Congress, or Stony Point. He was afraid to ask about any more friends, so he cried out, "Does nobody here know Rip Van Winkle?"

"Oh, Rip Van Winkle!" came the reply. "Oh, to be sure! That's Rip Van Winkle up there, leaning against the tree."

Rip looked and saw an exact copy of himself. Was he going crazy? He didn't know whether he was himself or another man. While he was trying to figure this out, the man in the three-cornered hat was asking, "Who are you? What is your name?"

"God only knows," Rip cried. "I'm not myself! I'm somebody else! That's me leaning against the tree—no—that's somebody else who's got into my shoes. I was myself last night, but I fell asleep on the mountain, and somebody's changed my gun. Everything's changed, and I'm changed, and I'm not sure what my name is, or who I am!"

The people began to look at each other, nod, wink, and tap their fingers against their foreheads. They whispered about grabbing Rip's gun to keep him from doing harm. At this tense moment, a woman with a nice face pushed through the crowd to get a peek at the gray-bearded man. She had a chubby child in her arms, who was frightened by the old man's looks and began to cry. "Be quiet, Rip," she cried. "The old man won't hurt you."

The name of the child, the face of the mother, the tone of her voice—all made Rip wonder. *Could it be?* "What is your name, my good woman?" he asked.

"Judith Gardenier."

"And your father's name?"

"Ah, poor man, Rip Van Winkle was his name, but it's been twenty years since he went away from home with his gun, and never has been heard of since. His dog came home without him. Whether he shot himself or was carried away by the Indians, nobody knows. I was just a little girl at that time."

Rip had only one question more to ask, but he asked it with a trembling voice.

"Where's your mother?"

"Oh, she too has died. She had a heart attack when she lost her temper and started scolding some peddler about his laziness."

This news saddened Rip almost as much as it surprised him. He got over it quickly and turned with a happy heart to hug his daughter and her child in his arms.

"I'm your father!" he cried. "Doesn't anybody here know poor Rip Van Winkle?"

All stood shocked, until an old woman came out from among the crowd. She stared into his face for a moment, and then cried, "Sure enough! It *is* Rip Van Winkle! Welcome home again, old neighbor. Why, where have you been these twenty long years?"

It did not take Rip long to tell his story, because, to him, the whole twenty years had been only one night. The neighbors just stared when they heard it. Some winked at each other and rolled their eyes. Soon they all began shaking their heads, for no one could believe the wild tale.

So they asked old Peter Vanderdonk what he thought about it. Peter was the oldest person of the village, and knew all the wonderful old stories that had been passed down over the years.

Peter remembered Rip right away and was able to explain his story. He told the group that it was a fact, handed down through history, that strange things had always haunted the Catskill Mountains. He also said that the ghost of Hendrick Hudson, the explorer who was the first to find the river and the lands around it, came back every twenty years, along with the crew of his ship, the *Half-Moon*. In this way, he was able to keep an eye on the great city, and the river named after him. Vanderdonk ended by saying that his father had once seen Hudson's men in their old Dutch clothing, playing at ninepins in a hollow of the mountain. In fact, he said, he himself had heard, one summer afternoon, the sound of their bowling balls, like distant crashes of thunder.

To make a long story short, the crowd broke up and began again to talk among themselves about the importance of voting in the election.

Rip's daughter took him home to live with her. She had a comfortable home, and a chubby, cheery farmer for a husband. Rip remembered him as one of the young rascals that used to climb upon his back.

Rip's son—who was that "exact copy of himself" Rip had seen leaning against the tree—was hired to work on the farm. He didn't like it much and took care of everybody else's business except his own—*like father, like son!*

# CHAPTER FOUR

# A Life of Freedom

Rip went back to his old way of life. He found many of his old pals and also started making friends with the younger people, who soon grew to like him.

He had nothing to do at home and had reached that happy age when a man could do as little as he pleased, so he spent most days telling stories on the bench in front of the inn. He became one of the most trusted men in the village. Everyone wanted to hear his history of what it was like "before the big war with England." It took Rip a long time to understand all the strange things that had happened during his twenty-year nap.

He eventually figured out that there had been a Revolutionary War. The country had fought for and won its freedom from England. Instead of a subject, being told what to do by His Majesty King George the Third, he was now a free citizen of the United States.

Rip wasn't too interested in such things. He didn't really understand them. But there was *one* kind of freedom that he *did* understand. That was freedom from scolding. He had won that freedom—not by fighting a long fight, but by sleeping a long sleep. He could now do as he chose, free of Her Majesty Mrs. Van Winkle. Whenever her name came up, he shook his head, shrugged his shoulders, and turned his eyes toward the heavens. No one was ever quite sure whether this was a sign of loneliness or one of thankfulness.

He used to tell his story to every stranger that arrived at Mr. Doolittle's hotel. At first, it changed a little with each telling, which was probably because of his long sleep. But after a while, his tale became the same each time, exactly as I have told it. Every man, woman, and child in the village knew it by heart. Some still wondered if it were true, and said that Rip might have been crazy.

But the old Dutch people of the village believed every word. Even now, when they hear a thunderstorm on a summer afternoon in the Catskill Mountains, they say that old Hendrick Hudson and his crew are having a game of ninepins. And all the hen-pecked husbands in the neighborhood, at the end of a hard day at home, wish that they might have a relaxing drink or two out of Rip Van Winkle's flagon.

## THE END

# THE SPECTRE BRIDEGROOM

# CONTENTS

# CHARACTERS

BARON — A German baron who lives in a castle

THE TWO AUNTS — the Baron's two sisters, who help raise his daughter

THE DAUGHTER — the Baron's lovely daughter

COUNT VON ALTENBURG — a young, handsome count, who is to marry the Baron's only daughter

HERMAN VON STARKENFAUST — the Count's friend (with the Count when he is murdered) whose family is feuding with the Baron

THE SPECTRE — the mysterious figure (a ghost?) who attends the wedding banquet and appears in the garden

# CHAPTER ONE

# The Baron Von Landshort

High on a hill in Germany, there once stood a castle. It was like a great eagle's nest that looked down over two large rivers. Only its tall watchtower now stands. The old, old castle has crumbled and fallen into decay.

At one time, it was the mighty home of Baron Von Landshort. He was from the family of Katzenellenbogen. (This used to be a rich and powerful family. The name means "Cat's Elbow," for the matron of the family had a very fine arm. This was how names came to be in those days.) The castle was passed on through the ages—until it was passed on to the Baron.

Many of the other barons left their crumbling castles to live in grand homes in town. But the Baron Von Landshort remained proudly in his castle on the hill. In fact, he rather enjoyed thinking that the old wars and feuds were still going on between families. Of course, there were no more wars. It was peacetime. But the Baron in the castle was foolish—and so he was not on good terms with his neighbors.

The Baron had only one child, a daughter— the apple of his eye. Now, two of the Baron's sisters knew just how a young noble lady should act and walk and speak. And so they raised the child and taught her everything they knew. By the time the girl was eighteen, she could read any history book. She could needlepoint so well her work made the people at court "Ooh" and "Aah." She was taught to dance and sing. She played the harp and guitar. And her arts and craft projects decorated the castle. *And*, she could even write her long last name—*Von Landshort of the family of Katzenellenbogen*—without missing a letter! Everyone told the Baron what a splendid daughter he had—of course.

The girl was taught proper manners, proper curtsies, and the proper way to be around men. And this, the aunts said, was "to *not* be around them at all!" The two aunts had been *terrible* flirts in their day, and told her never to even look at a man. (Even if one of the handsomest knights were dying at her feet!) The aunts didn't let her out of their sight. And this is what comes from being raised by two aunts who had been terrible flirts in their day.

These lessons worked well. The young lady was sweet, very nice, and polite. She bloomed into a rosebud, carefully tended by her aunts. Her aunts looked upon her with pride and happiness. "Let all the other young ladies in the world go astray," they said. "Thank Heaven, nothing of the kind could happen to this young lady!"

The Baron had only one child, but he had a rather large household. He had been blessed with many poor relatives, and they were all very attached to him. They often came in swarms to "liven up the castle." They met for family festivals and family feasts—and the Baron had to pay for it all. These relatives said there was *nothing* on earth so delightful as these family "meetings."

The Baron was a small man, but he had a big heart. It swelled with pride at being the greatest man in the little world about him. He loved to tell long stories about the warriors who were pictured in the castle. His poor relatives listened with much interest. He told ghost stories and strange tales of old. Everyone listened in wonder with open eyes and mouth. No matter how many times the Baron told a story, his relatives hung onto every word (while they hung onto every turkey leg and goblet).

Thus lived the Baron Von Landshort, the "king" and "wisest man" in his little world.

# CHAPTER TWO

# Marriage Plans—and Murder

It so happened that at this time there was a great family gathering at the castle. They were there to meet the future bridegroom of the Baron's daughter. The Baron had made an agreement with an old nobleman of Bavaria. They would unite their families through the marriage of their children. The young people were thus engaged to be married—without ever seeing each other! And the time was set for the wedding.

The young Count Von Altenburg, the groom, had been called away from the army. He was now on his way to the castle to meet his bride, and attend his own wedding.

The castle was very busy getting ready for the Count. The fair bride had been decked out with great care. The two aunts fussed over her hair, her jewelry, and her clothes, until she was quite lovely. They told her how to walk, how to hold her hands just so, and what to say to her young groom.

The Baron was also bustling about the castle, from top to bottom. He called out orders to the servants. He buzzed about every hall and chamber, like a bluebottle fly on a warm day.

In the meantime, a great banquet was made ready. The kitchen was crowded with good cheer. The best bottles of wine were brought from the cellar. The finest German orchestra was ready to play. Everything was ready to receive the grand guest in style.

But the guest did not show up.

Hour rolled after hour. The sun began to set behind the mountains. The Baron mounted the highest tower and strained his eyes in hope of seeing the Count and his attendants. One time he thought he saw them. He heard horns and saw horsemen far down the road. However, they went off in a different direction.

The last ray of sunshine departed. The bats began to flit by in the twilight. The road grew dimmer and dimmer to the view. And nothing appeared on the road except here and there a weary farmhand returning home.

While the old castle of Landshort waited and wondered, a very interesting scene was taking place in a different part of Germany.

The young Count Von Altenburg was trotting along with a light heart on the road to the Baron's castle. He was lazily dreaming of the young, beautiful bride and the great dinner that awaited him. Along the way, in Wurtzburg, he came upon a war buddy of his—Herman Von Starkenfaust. The Count gave him a hearty greeting. For his friend was one of the bravest, most worthy men he knew.

The two young friends caught up on news. The Count said he was on his way to his own wedding. He explained that he had never met the young lady, but she was said to be charming and lovely.

The two friends were going in the same direction. Herman's father's castle was not far from the Baron's (although a feud had kept the families apart). The Count and Herman decided to journey together.

"Let's leave early tomorrow morning," said the Count to his friend. "I'll tell my court to start later and catch up to us. That way we'll have some time alone to talk about old times and new fortunes to be made."

Just before daybreak, the two set off. They whiled away the time talking about their adventures in the army. And, of course, the Count wanted to discuss his new bride and marriage, as any nervous bridegroom would.

In this way, they had come to the mountains of the Odenwald. Here they had to cross a lonely and thickly wooded pass. It was well known at that time that the forests of Germany were infested with robbers. And these fine gentlemen were attacked by a gang of bandits in the midst of the forest. They defended themselves bravely, but were nearly overpowered. When the Count's attendants arrived, the robbers fled. But the Count had been badly wounded.

The Count's attendants slowly and carefully carried him back to the city of Wurtzburg. A priest was called. With his dying breath, the Count begged his friend, Herman, to go immediately to the castle of Landshort.

"Tell them," he gasped, "tell them I cannot come—can never come. Unless this is done, I shall not sleep quietly in my grave!"

Herman promised to fulfill this dying wish, and gave him his hand in solemn pledge. The dying man shook his hand, and then gasped his last breath.

Herman sighed deeply. His tears fell as he bent over his comrade—a fallen soldier—a dear friend. His heart was heavy, but he thought over this mission. He was from a family that was feuding with the Baron. His friend had asked him to show up at this great party as an uninvited, unwanted guest. And then he would have to give them the awful news. But he had made a promise. And he had shaken on that pledge.

And so he arranged for the Count to be buried in the cathedral of Wurtzburg. He left the funeral in the hands of the Count's attendants, and made ready for his journey to the Baron's castle.

# CHAPTER THREE

# The Bridegroom Arrives

It is now time to return to the old family of Katzenellenbogen who were waiting for their guest—and their dinner.

Night closed in, but still no guest arrived. The Baron came down from the tower in despair. The banquet had been delayed hour upon hour. The meats were overdone. The cook was in agony. All the family members looked as if they were starving. The Baron sadly gave the order for the feast to begin. All were seated at the grand tables. And just as they were about to start, they heard the sound of a horn outside the gate. Another long blast filled the castle with its echoes.

The guest had arrived! The Baron quickly went to receive his future son-in-law.

The drawbridge had been let down, and the stranger was before the gate. He was a tall, gallant knight, mounted on a black steed. His face was pale, but he had a beaming, stately eye. The Baron was a little ruffled that he had come alone, with no attendants.

"I am sorry," said the stranger, "to break in upon you at this late hour—"

"Think nothing of it, my good, noble man! Come in! Come in!" cried the Baron. He went on and on about how delighted he was.

The stranger could not say a word. He simply bowed his head and followed the Baron into the castle. By the time they had reached the inner court, the stranger tried again to speak. But here the ladies flew forward, pushing the blushing bride before them—and then he *surely* could not speak. He gazed on her for a moment as if he were in a trance. One of the old aunts whispered something in her ear, and the young lady made an effort to speak. She gave a shy glance with her blue eyes, then cast them to the ground. There was a sweet smile playing about her lips, and a soft dimpling of the cheek. For this young man was truly handsome and gallant.

Because it was so late, the banquet was begun at once! It was served up in the great hall of the castle. All around hung paintings of past heroes, and crests, and spears and banners. Yet the young man took little notice of the room, or the other guests, or even the food. He seemed absorbed in admiration of his bride. He spoke with her in a low tone that no one else could hear—for the language of love is never loud. The young lady hung onto every word. Now and then she made some blushing reply. And when his eye was turned away, she would steal a sidelong glance at his romantic face, and heave a gentle sigh of tender happiness. It was clear that the young couple was completely in love. The aunts declared that the two had fallen in love with each other at first sight.

The feast went on merrily. The Baron told his best and longest stories. All the guests listened with astonishment, and laughed at exactly the right place. There were songs and witty jokes and merry-making the night through.

Only the stranger seemed to remain quiet—and strangely serious. His face grew more downcast as the evening wore on. Even the Baron's jokes seemed only to make him more sad. At times he looked lost in thought. Quietly, mysteriously, and earnestly, he talked with his bride. Lowering clouds began to steal over her fair face. And didn't she seem to shiver at times?

All this could not escape the notice of the company. Their celebration was chilled by the strange gloom of the bridegroom. They whispered, exchanged glances, shrugged their shoulders, and shook their heads. The singing died away. The laughter faded. There were dreary pauses in the conversation. The room grew deathly quiet—and this, of course, led to the telling of ghost stories. One dismal story led to another dismal story. The Baron nearly frightened some of the ladies into fits with the tale of the goblin horseman that carried away a fair maiden.

The bridegroom turned to listen now with great attention. He kept his eyes fixed on the Baron. As the story drew to a close, he slowly, slowly rose from his seat. The moment the tale was finished, he heaved a deep sigh—and bid farewell to all.

Everyone stared in amazement. The Baron was perfectly thunderstruck.

"What? Leaving now? At midnight? Why, we've prepared everything for the wedding tomorrow. If you are tired, your chamber is ready—"

The stranger shook his head mournfully and mysteriously. "I must lay my head in a different chamber tonight."

Waving his farewell to the company, he stalked slowly out of the hall. The two old aunts were in shock. The bride hung her head, and a tear stole to her eye.

The Baron followed the stranger to the great court of the castle. There the black horse stood, snorting and pawing the earth. When they had reached the arched gate, dimly lit by a torch, the stranger paused. He turned to the Baron and spoke in a hollow tone of voice. His words echoed off the vaulted ceiling—as if in a tomb.

"Now that we are alone," he said, "I will tell why I must go. I have a solemn appointment—"

"Can't you send someone in your place?" asked the Baron.

"No. I must attend it in person—I must get to Wurtzburg cathedral—"

"Ah, yes!" said the Baron, plucking up spirit. "For the wedding! But not until tomorrow! Tomorrow you shall take your bride there."

"No! No!" wailed the stranger. "My appointment is with no bride… The worms! The worms expect me! I am a dead man—I have been killed by robbers—My body lies at Wurtzburg! At midnight I am to be buried—The grave is waiting for me—I must keep my appointment!"

He sprang onto his black horse and dashed over the drawbridge. The horse's hooves clattered off and away into the night.

# CHAPTER FOUR

# The Spectre in the Garden

The Baron returned to the hall quite shaken. He told the entire company what the stranger had said. Two ladies fainted right away. Others were sickened that they had eaten with a spectre—a ghost in human form. Some said this might be the wild huntsman, famous in German legend. Some talked of mountain spirits, of wood-demons, and of other ghostly beings.

The next day, messengers brought the final word. Indeed the young Count *had* been murdered. He had been buried at midnight in Wurtzburg cathedral.

You can imagine the dismay at the castle!

The Baron shut himself up in his chamber. The guests wandered about the courts, or collected in groups in the hall. They shook their heads and shrugged their shoulders at the troubles of so good a man. But the widowed bride was the most pitiful. Oh, to lose a husband before the first embrace— and such a husband! If his ghost was so gracious and noble, the living man must have been even *more* gracious and noble! She filled the house with her sad sobbing.

Two days after the ghostly visit, the young lady had gone early to her chamber. One of her aunts insisted on staying with her. Now, this aunt was one of the best tellers of ghost stories in all Germany. So she passed the time telling one of her longest to her niece—but fell asleep in the middle of it. The niece lay gazing at moonbeams shining through her one window. The castle clock had just struck midnight, when a soft strain of music drifted up from the garden beneath her window. She rose quickly from her bed and stepped lightly to the window. A tall figure stood among the shadows of the trees. As it raised its head, a beam of moonlight fell upon the face. Heaven and earth! She beheld the Spectre Bridegroom!

A loud shriek at that moment burst upon her ear. Her aunt, who had been awakened by the music and had followed her silently to the window, fell into her arms. When she looked again, the spectre had disappeared.

The aunt was beside herself with terror. The young lady, however, said her heart went out even to—this—this spectre of her beloved. The aunt declared she herself would never sleep in that chamber again.

"I'll sleep in no other chamber in the castle!" declared the niece.

And so the young lady had to sleep in the room alone. She made her aunt promise not to tell the story of the spectre. "Otherwise," she said, "my father will not allow me to stay here. And then I could never see the ghost—who holds my heart."

# CHAPTER FIVE

# And So the Story Ends

The girl's aunt actually kept her promise a whole week! But, as everyone knows, it is so hard to keep a secret if you're the first to be able to tell a frightful story. And so, one morning at breakfast, she blurted the whole thing out—how a spectre had appeared outside the girl's window! And what made her tell? News was brought to the table that the young lady was not to be found. Her room was empty—the bed had not been slept in—the window was open, and the "bird" had flown! The aunt was first speechless. Then she wrung her hands and shrieked, "The goblin! The goblin! She's carried away by the goblin."

In a few words she related the fearful scene of the garden. Everyone agreed that the spectre must have carried off his bride. Two of the maids said they had heard the clattering of horse hooves down the mountain about midnight. They had no doubt it was the spectre on his black horse, taking her away to the tomb. (Some people were not surprised at the news. These things were common in Germany back then, you see.)

What a sad situation for the poor Baron! What a heart-breaking problem for a fond father, and a member of the great family of Katzenellenbogen! His only daughter had either been stolen away to the grave, or he was to have some wood-demon for a son-in-law. And—horrors! Would he have a troop of goblin grandchildren?

The Baron was quite upset and confused, and all the castle was in an uproar. The men were ordered to search every road and path and glen of the area. The Baron himself put on his jack-boots and strapped on his sword. He was about to mount his horse to go seek his daughter, when he stopped suddenly. Someone was approaching the castle.

# THE SPECTRE BRIDEGROOM

❧ 180 ❧

Here came a young lady and a knight, both on horseback. The lady galloped up to the gate and sprang from her horse. She fell at the Baron's feet and embraced his knees. It was his lost daughter! And her companion—the Spectre Bridegroom!

The Baron was astounded. He looked at his daughter, then at the spectre. Could he believe his senses? The young man looked much better than when he had said farewell to the Baron that night to go off to the world of spirits. His outfit was splendid. In fact, he was quite a noble and manly figure. He was no longer pale and sad-looking. His fine face was rosy and his dark eyes were alight with joy.

The mystery was soon cleared up. The knight (for, as you must have known all the while, he was no goblin) announced himself as Sir Herman Von Starkenfaust. He then told his story.

He had met the Count, his friend, who was killed soon after. He had hurried to the castle to deliver the bad news. He had tried to tell the Baron, but the Baron had interrupted him over and over and led him into the great banquet hall. And there he had seen the bride—the lovely bride! He had fallen in love with her at first sight.

He wanted to tell the news of the Count, but instead he sat with the young lady and let everyone believe he was the groom. He did not know how he would get out of the lie—until the Baron began telling goblin stories. This gave him the idea to claim he was the ghost of the Count— and to ride off into the night. However, that could not be the end of his troubles, for he found himself sorely in love with the young lady. And how could he face the Baron and tell him now? After all, his own family and the Baron's family were having a feud! So, instead, he would sneak at night into the garden beneath the young lady's window. There he told the lady of his undying love, night after night. He won her heart—and one night, he whisked her away and the two were happily married.

The Baron should have been angry! Outraged! Furious! A member of a feuding family with his daughter? However, the good Baron loved his daughter and rejoiced to find her still alive. Yes, this young man was from an "enemy house," but he was not a goblin, at least. Yes, the man had lied about being a dead man, but it was all for love— and all is fair in love and war, they say.

And so, the Baron forgave the young couple on the spot. The castle threw a party and a banquet (which thrilled all the relatives who were still living at the castle). Everyone welcomed this new member of the family with loving kindness. He was so gallant, so generous—and so rich! One of the aunts was a bit upset that the *only* spectre she had ever seen turned out to be a real man. But the niece seemed perfectly happy that he turned out to be a real man—and so the story ends.

## THE END

# ABOUT THE AUTHOR

## WASHINGTON IRVING

Washington Irving was born in 1783 in New York, the youngest of eleven children. He was named after General George Washington. From an early age, Irving was an avid reader and imaginative writer. Even after he began to practice law, he wrote for newspapers and magazines as a fun side-job.

In 1809, Irving published *Knickerbocker's History of New York*, a witty, well-written collection of humorous tales. It became popular with American and British readers alike.

Irving moved to England in 1815 to help handle his family's import-export business. In 1817 the business failed, so Irving took up his pen to earn a living. In 1819, he released *The Sketch Book of Geoffrey Crayon, Gent.* which included "The Legend of Sleepy Hollow" and "Rip Van Winkle." Many stories and essays followed, including "The Spectre Bridegroom," which met with great success.

Irving died in 1859. He has since been declared the "Father of American Literature." After nearly 200 years, his witty style, mastery of language, colorful characters, and amusing stories are still enjoyable and popular.